MIAMI HEAT

by Marty Gitlin

Published by ABDO Publishing Company, 8000 West 78th Street, Edina, Minnesota 55439. Copyright © 2012 by Abdo Consulting Group, Inc. International copyrights reserved in all countries. No part of this book may be reproduced in any form without written permission from the publisher. SportsZone™ is a trademark and logo of ABDO Publishing Company.

Printed in the United States of America,
North Mankato, Minnesota
062011
092011

 THIS BOOK CONTAINS AT LEAST 10% RECYCLED MATERIALS.

Editor: Alex Monnig
Copy Editor: Anna Comstock
Series design: Christa Schneider
Cover production: Craig Hinton
Interior production: Carol Castro

Photo Credits: Mark J. Terrill/AP Images, cover; Rusty Kennedy/AP Images, 1; Lynne Sladky/AP Images, 4, 36; J. Pat Carter/AP Images, 7; Eric Gay/AP Images, 8; Jim Mone/AP Images, 10; Kathy Willens/AP Images, 13, 27, 43 (top); Mark Elias/AP Images, 14, 42 (top); Hans Deryk/AP Images, 16, 42 (bottom); Jeffrey Boan/AP Images, 19, 42 (middle); Rick Bowmer/AP Images, 20; Wilfredo Lee/AP Images, 23, 24, 31; Amy E. Conn/AP Images, 28; Alan Diaz/AP Images, 32, 43 (middle), 44, 47; John F. Martin/AP Images, 35; Jeff Daly/PictureGroup/AP Images, 39, 43 (bottom); Lucy Nicholson/AP Images, 41

Library of Congress Cataloging-in-Publication Data
Gitlin, Marty.
  Miami Heat / by Marty Gitlin.
      p. cm. -- (Inside the NBA)
  Includes index.
  ISBN 978-1-61783-163-8
  1. Miami Heat (Basketball team)--History--Juvenile literature. I. Title.
  GV885.52.M53G58 2012
  796.323'6409759381--dc23
                                        2011022353

TABLE OF CONTENTS

Chapter 1 .... Return From the Dead, 4

Chapter 2 .... The Bad Old Days, 10

Chapter 3 .... "Knicking" Each Other Up, 16

Chapter 4 .... New Home, New Frustrations, 24

Chapter 5 .... Help for Wade: "The Decision," 32

Timeline, 42

Quick Stats, 44

Quotes and Anecdotes, 45

Glossary, 46

For More Information, 47

Index, 48

About the Author, 48

CHAPTER 1

RETURN FROM THE DEAD

The Miami Heat had one foot in the grave, and the Dallas Mavericks were about to push them in. The Heat appeared doomed in the 2006 National Basketball Association (NBA) Finals.

They had lost in Game 1 when they scored just 12 points in the fourth quarter. They lost in Game 2 when they were outscored 27–6 to end the first half. And they were trailing by 13 points midway through the fourth quarter in Game 3.

The clock was ticking down to its final seconds. And with it drained all hope for a championship.

Not at Their Peak? Who Cares?

Every NBA team hopes to be playing their best basketball going into the playoffs. But the Heat, unfortunately, were playing their worst in 2006. They had lost three straight games and seven of their last 11. Yet they bounced back to win the championship. That season, the Heat performed their best after Pat Riley replaced Stan Van Gundy as coach in December of 2005. They won 34 of their next 45 games.

Dwyane Wade (3) shoots over Dallas Mavericks defender Adrian Griffin in Game 5 of the 2006 NBA Finals. The Heat won 101–100 in overtime.

RETURN FROM THE DEAD

But suddenly the Heat began to fight back. Young superstar guard Dwyane Wade led the way. He hit a 15-foot jump shot. He hit a layup. He hit a 17-foot jump shot. He hit another layup. He hit a 20-foot jump shot that cut the Dallas lead to 93–92. And with just nine seconds remaining, Heat point guard Gary Payton nailed a 21-foot jump shot to give Miami a 97–95 lead.

They needed one defensive stop to win the game. It seemed only appropriate that Wade stole the ball to clinch the victory and save the season. He finished the game with 42 points and 13 rebounds. "We never gave up," Heat center Shaquille O'Neal said. "We just kept playing, showed a lot of heart, a lot of intensity."

They showed a lot of intensity the rest of the series as well. Wade was not through playing the role of hero. He scored 36 points in a 98–74 Heat victory in Game 4. And he added 43 points, including two game-winning foul shots with one second left, in Miami's 101–100 Game 5 triumph.

Once again in Game 6, the Heat faced an uphill climb. They fell behind by 14 points in the first quarter. But Miami outplayed the Mavericks the

> **End of a Great Career**
>
> When veteran point guard Gary Payton joined the Heat in 2005, he played in every game but one and helped contribute to the championship run. Before he came to Miami, Payton averaged at least 19 points and seven assists per game for nine straight seasons starting in 1994–95. Payton earned a spot on the Western Conference All-Star team nine times. And he was considered one of the top defensive players in the game. Besides Miami, Payton played for the Seattle SuperSonics, the Milwaukee Bucks, the Boston Celtics, and the Los Angeles Lakers.

Gary Payton, *right*, hits the game-winning shot in Game 3 of the 2006 NBA Finals against the Dallas Mavericks.

rest of the way and went on to win 95–92 to secure their first title. Wade finished Game 6 with 36 points and 10 rebounds. He was named the NBA Finals Most Valuable Player (MVP).

While the Heat players and fans celebrated, Wade

RETURN FROM THE DEAD

exclaimed, "I don't want to say I put this team on my back." But coach Pat Riley knew Wade had done just that. "He just took it to another level," Riley said. "He's making a legacy in his third year. Dwyane's probably one of the most respected young players this game has had in a long time."

Fans were excited about Wade and the rest of the team's future. They were determined to put the past behind them. It was a past that started with the franchise's creation 19 years earlier and included a stretch during which Miami was the worst team in the league.

Shaquille O'Neal tries to score during Game 1 of the 2006 NBA Finals against the Dallas Mavericks.

CHAMPIONSHIP COACH

Pat Riley had coached in the NBA for 13 years before he landed in Miami in 1995. Each of his teams had won at least 50 games. In the 1980s, he guided the Los Angeles Lakers to four NBA championships, including one in his first season in 1982. He coached the New York Knicks for four seasons and led them to an Eastern Conference title in 1994. Riley coached 24 total years in the league before retiring in 2008. In 20 of those years, his teams finished first or second in their division.

"There's always the motivation of wanting to win," he said. "Everybody has that. But a champion needs, in his attitude, a motivation above and beyond winning."

Riley was named NBA Coach of the Year in 1990, 1993, and 1997. Through the 2010–11 season, he ranked fourth in NBA history with 1,210 coaching victories.

RETURN FROM THE DEAD 9

CHAPTER 2

THE BAD OLD DAYS

NBA expansion teams usually have difficulty winning in their first few seasons. But few could have imagined that the Heat would have as much trouble as they did when they entered the league.

The Heat franchise was founded in 1987 when the NBA decided to add four new teams. Miami began play in 1988 along with the Charlotte Hornets. The Orlando Magic and the Minnesota Timberwolves joined the league the following year.

The Heat team was stocked with inexperienced rookies and veterans who had not achieved much in the NBA. They lost their first game by 20 points and then continued to lose. They even lost one game by 47 points to the Los Angeles Lakers. Before Miami claimed its first victory, it owned a record of 0–17. It was the worst start in league history.

The constant failure had the Heat wondering if they were

Heat guard Sherman Douglas, *left*, tries to pass during a December 1989 game against the Minnesota Timberwolves.

THE BAD OLD DAYS 11

CREATING THE HEAT

Billy Cunningham helped bring an NBA team to Miami. He was not only a part owner of the Heat, but he was also a Hall of Fame player and coach. During his playing career in the 1960s and 1970s, Cunningham was a forward for the Philadelphia 76ers. His jumping ability earned him the nickname "The Kangaroo Kid." He averaged 20.8 points and 10.1 rebounds per game during his time in the NBA. He peaked in the 1969–70 season when he recorded career highs of 26.1 points and 13.6 rebounds per game.

After retiring as a player, Cunningham coached the 76ers for eight seasons and guided them to a championship in 1983. He left coaching to become an NBA analyst on CBS television in 1985. He was elected to the Hall of Fame in 1986 before taking part ownership of the Heat. Cunningham sold his share of the team in 1995.

ever going to win a game. "I guess the worst thing I think about is—what else?—actually going 0–82," Heat coach Ron Rothstein said after his team lost its first 16 games. "You look at the schedule and think, well, who are we going to beat? And when?"

But despite all of the losses, there was reason for hope. The Heat had selected talented players in the NBA Draft. Center Rony Seikaly and guard Kevin Edwards showed potential. And the team's 15–67 record their first year allowed them to grab future star forward Glen Rice and quick guard Sherman Douglas in the 1989 NBA Draft.

The promising youth did not translate into victories during the Heat's second season, though. Individually, they shined. Seikaly averaged

Glen Rice, *left*, grabs a rebound against the Orlando Magic's Greg Kite during a 1990 game.

17 points and 10 rebounds per game to win the NBA Most Improved Player Award. And Douglas was named to the All-Rookie first team. But the Heat still won just 18 games. They suffered through one losing streak of 13 games and two more of nine games each. They never won more than two games in a row.

Rapid Rise

The Heat won only a combined 33 games during their first two seasons. But they still reached the playoffs faster than the other three expansion teams of their era. It took them just four years to qualify. The Charlotte Hornets and the Orlando Magic both made the playoffs in their fifth seasons. The Minnesota Timberwolves did not get in until their eighth year in the NBA.

Steve Smith (3) goes to the hoop against the Chicago Bulls during Game 1 of the first round of the 1992 playoffs. The Heat lost 113–94.

Douglas, Rice, and Seikaly continued to grow on the court during the 1990–91 season. But the team still finished its third year with a record of 24–58. The Heat again had trouble halting losing streaks. Miami dropped 10 in a row early in the season. They later lost eight straight and finished the season losing nine of their last 11 games.

The Heat owned a three-year record of 57–189. That was enough losing for Rothstein, who quit in 1991. He was replaced by experienced NBA coach Kevin Loughery.

Miami continued to stockpile young talent. In the 1991 NBA Draft, they picked high-scoring guard Steve Smith. At 6 feet 6 inches, Smith towered over many of the other guards

> ### Home, Sweet Home
>
> NBA teams almost always sport better records at home than they do on the road. The Heat were no different during the 1991–92 season. They finished with a 28–13 record at Miami Arena that year. But they stumbled to a 10–31 mark away from home. Most teams that lose more than they win do not make the playoffs. But the Heat qualified that year despite a 38–44 record.

in the NBA. The Heat believed the combination of Smith and Rice would transform them into a playoff contender.

They were right. What had been the worst team in basketball suddenly started to win. Rice became a scoring machine. In April 1992, he scored 46 points in one game against Orlando. He combined for 70 points in two other games the same week. He was named NBA Player of the Month.

The Heat battled the Atlanta Hawks for the eighth and final playoff spot in the Eastern Conference. When the Hawks lost to the Cleveland Cavaliers on the last day of the regular season, the Heat snuck into the postseason with a 38–44 record. They were eliminated after losing three straight games to superstar Michael Jordan and the powerful Chicago Bulls in the first round, but things were looking up for Miami.

The first four years of Heat basketball did not result in many wins. But Miami did improve its record every season. In 1991, a poll of NBA team executives in *Sports Illustrated* predicted Miami would be the most successful of the four recent expansion teams. The Heat were improving. But their goal of competing for an NBA championship would have to wait a few more years.

THE BAD OLD DAYS   **15**

CHAPTER 3

"KNICKING" EACH OTHER UP

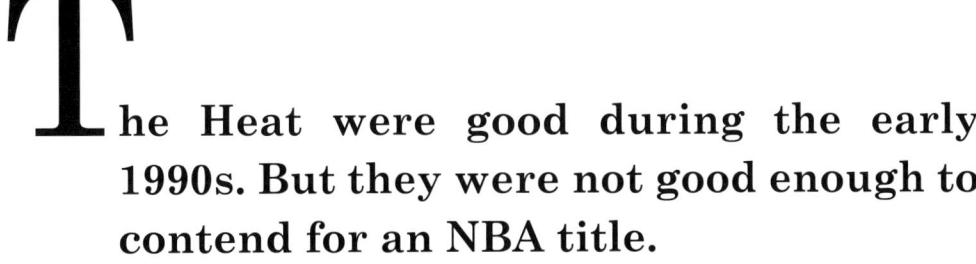

T he Heat were good during the early 1990s. But they were not good enough to contend for an NBA title.

After a knee injury to Steve Smith contributed to a poor 1992–93 season, the Heat turned their fortunes around. They finished the next year with their best record up to that point. At 42–40, they qualified for the postseason. They even won their first playoff game when they beat the Atlanta Hawks.

But the Heat went on to lose the series to the Hawks. Owner Mickey Arison decided it was time for major changes. He traded Smith and original Heat players Rony Seikaly and Grant Long. He also acquired

Tim Hardaway, *left*, drives to the hoop during Game 2 of the Heat's 1997 second-round playoff series against the New York Knicks. The Heat won 88–84.

"KNICKING" EACH OTHER UP **17**

TIM TERRIFIC

Tim Hardaway was only 6 feet tall, which is tiny by NBA standards. But he was so quick that he was nicknamed "The Bug." Before he joined the Heat in 1996, Hardaway spent his time leading the fast-paced Golden State Warriors. He was named to the NBA All-Rookie team in 1990. Over the next four seasons, he averaged at least 20 points and between 9.3 and 10.6 assists per game every season for Golden State. Hardaway was named to the Western Conference All-Star team three times with the Warriors.

He remained effective in Miami, but was limited by injuries. In five-plus years with the Heat, Hardaway averaged between 13.4 and 20.3 points, and 6.3 and 10 assists per game. He also earned two more trips to the All-Star Game. Through the 2010–11 season, Hardaway was 13th on the all-time NBA career list in assists with 7,095.

talented forward Kevin Willis. He promoted Kevin Loughery to a front-office position and named Alvin Gentry the new head coach.

The moves backfired. The Heat won just 32 games the next season. Willis and Glen Rice combined to average nearly 40 points a game, but they received little help from their teammates. So the Heat made even bolder moves in 1995, including the hiring of new coach Pat Riley.

The day before the 1995–96 season began, Miami traded Rice and two other players to the Charlotte Hornets. They received three players in return, one of whom was top center Alonzo Mourning. Riley had coached Hall of Fame center Patrick Ewing while with the New York Knicks. Now he wanted to build his offense and defense

Alonzo Mourning joined the Heat in 1995 and helped lead them to the Eastern Conference finals just a season later.

around Mourning. That overhaul was just the beginning. Three months later, the Heat traded for five more players, including speedy guard Tim Hardaway.

Although it took some time for all the new players to mesh on the court, Riley coached

'Mourning' a Loss

One reason the Heat lost to the New York Knicks in the 1998 playoffs was because center Alonzo Mourning did not play in the fifth and final game. Mourning was healthy, but he got into a fight with the Knicks' Larry Johnson in Game 4 and was suspended for Game 5. Mourning was missed. The Heat lost 98–81.

"KNICKING" EACH OTHER UP 19

Jamal Mashburn was hampered by injuries during his four seasons with the Heat.

Miami into the playoffs. They were swept in the first round by the Chicago Bulls, but they were about to blossom into a title contender.

Hardaway and Mourning would lead the way. During the 1996–97 season, Hardaway finished fourth in the NBA MVP voting. He led the team with

> **Battered Mashburn**
>
> The Heat believed forward Jamal Mashburn would be a huge help when they traded for him in 1997. After all, he had averaged nearly 24 points per game with the Dallas Mavericks during the previous two seasons. But Mashburn was not able to help the Heat much. Due to injury, he played fewer than half the games from 1997 to 1999. He missed 34 games his first full year in Miami with a broken thumb. He missed 58 games the next season with a thigh injury.

20.3 points and 8.6 assists per game. Mourning contributed nearly 20 points and 10 rebounds per game. He also placed fourth in the league in blocked shots.

The Heat won 19 more games than they ever had in a season. They finished 61–21 to take the Atlantic Division title.

And this time they were not overwhelmed when the playoffs rolled around. They won their first playoff series by beating the Orlando Magic in the first round. The Heat then fell behind the New York Knicks three games to one in the second round. But Miami won the next two games, and then led Game 7 from beginning to end to win the series. Hardaway and Mourning combined for 60 points in the victory.

Riley had not only guided the Heat into the Eastern Conference finals. He had beaten his former Knicks team in the process. Some Knicks fans who were unhappy with him back when he coached their team called him "Pat the Rat." But Riley stressed that he did not feel any "special joy" in eliminating New York. "I'm a happy rat right now, okay?" said Riley. "Not for any reason other than I'm happy to move on [in the playoffs]."

But nobody was about to move on against Michael Jordan

> **Laying Down Some 'D'**
>
> The 1998–99 Heat did not score a lot of points, but they made up for it with a stifling defense. They gave up an average of just 84 points per game. They were ranked second in the NBA defensively. The Heat surrendered 100 points or more just five times that season. They peaked on April 10 when they yielded just 49 points to the Chicago Bulls. It was the lowest point total scored by one team in the modern era of the NBA. The Bulls made just 18 of 77 shots in that game.

and the Chicago Bulls. The Heat managed to win one game against Chicago. However, the Bulls eventually advanced to the Finals and won their second consecutive championship. It was their fifth in seven seasons.

The following season, Heat fans who had assumed their team was on the way to the top were disappointed. The Knicks got revenge for their loss in the 1997 playoffs by beating the Heat in the first round of the postseason in both 1998 and 1999.

Miami had the best record in the Eastern Conference in 1998–99. Mourning averaged 20 points and 11 rebounds per game to finish second in the MVP voting.

That season, they were expected to beat the Knicks in the first round of the playoffs. But the two rivals split the first four games. The Heat led the Knicks 77–76 late in the deciding Game 5. But with time running out, Knicks guard Allan Houston launched a running one-handed shot from 14 feet away. The ball bounced off the rim, kissed off the backboard, and fell through the net. The buzzer sounded a New York victory.

The screaming crowd at Miami Arena turned dead silent. Mourning left the court with a scowl on his face.

The Knicks' Allan Houston, *right*, hits the game-winning basket during Game 5 of the first round of the 1999 playoffs, while Miami forward P. J. Brown looks on.

"For it to come down to this kind of makes you angry a little bit," he said. "Regardless of the outcome, I still feel we're a better team than they are."

But in the NBA, a team must prove they are better by winning in the playoffs. And until the arrivals of Dwyane Wade and Shaquille O'Neal, the Heat would not win enough to earn a championship.

"KNICKING" EACH OTHER UP 23

CHAPTER 4

NEW HOME, NEW FRUSTRATIONS

January 1, 2000, was not just the beginning of a new millennium. It also marked the beginning of a new era for the Heat. That was the day they moved into their new home.

Nearly 20,000 fans packed AmericanAirlines Arena to watch their favorite team beat the Orlando Magic. They would witness many more victories that season. The Heat won 18 of 26 games during one stretch late in 2000. And they swept the Detroit Pistons in the first round of the playoffs.

The Heat appeared to be clicking on all cylinders heading into yet another showdown with the New York Knicks. Miami had finished the 1999–2000 season with a 52–30 record to beat out the Knicks for the Atlantic Division title. Mourning had been dominant. He placed third in the MVP

Alonzo Mourning, *left*, and Jamal Mashburn (24) were the top two scorers for the Heat during the 1999–2000 season.

BETTER MAN THAN PLAYER

For all of the great things Alonzo Mourning did on the basketball court, he was also well known for his generosity off of it.

A kidney disorder forced the Heat center to take a kidney transplant from his cousin in 2003. The surgery motivated Mourning to start the Alonzo Mourning Charities, which raise money for groups that help abused and neglected children. Through 2011, he has also raised more than $7 million for kidney research and medicine for families that cannot afford it.

USA Weekend magazine gave Mourning and tennis player Andre Agassi its Most Caring Athlete Award in 2001. Mourning and wife Tracy host an annual holiday party in which they give gifts to 400 foster children. They also distribute Thanksgiving meals to the needy.

voting after averaging nearly 22 points and 10 rebounds per game.

Revenge against New York was on the minds of Mourning and his teammates. They had been eliminated in the playoffs by the Knicks the previous two years.

The second-round series was once again a tight defensive struggle. Only once did either team score more than 87 points. Three of the seven games were decided by two points or less. And no margin of victory was greater than eight points. The heated rivals split the first six games. Only the winner of Game 7 would remain alive in the quest for an NBA championship.

Tim Hardaway nailed a three-pointer with 1:32 left on the clock to give the Heat an 82–81 lead. Knicks future Hall of Fame center Patrick Ewing

Anthony Carter, *left*, drives past Charlie Ward of the New York Knicks in the Heat's 77–76 Game 3 victory in the second round of the 2000 playoffs.

answered with a slam dunk to put his team ahead 83–82.

Then one of the most controversial endings in playoff history began to take shape. The Heat missed two shots but got the ball back with 12 seconds remaining. A shot by Heat forward Clarence Weatherspoon hit off the rim and was rebounded by Knicks guard Latrell Sprewell with two seconds left.

The Heat wanted to foul Sprewell to stop the clock. That would allow them to get the ball back after Sprewell took two foul shots. But the referee claimed

NEW HOME, NEW FRUSTRATIONS 27

Anthony Mason (14) drives against P. J. Brown of the Charlotte Hornets in Game 2 of the first round of the 2001 playoffs.

End of an Era

A remarkable run by coach Pat Riley ended in 2002. That was the year his Heat finished with a 36–46 record. Riley had coached 19 straight playoff teams until that season. He coached the Los Angeles Lakers to nine straight playoff berths. He also took the New York Knicks to four postseasons in a row before leading Miami to six consecutive playoff appearances.

Sprewell called a timeout. The Heat protested, arguing that a timeout was never called. Even Sprewell admitted after the game that he had never called the timeout.

The final two seconds ticked off the clock when Sprewell tossed the ball to teammate Charlie Ward, who

> ### Special Occasion
>
> Bob McAdoo never played for the Heat. But he did receive quite an honor during the time he was their assistant coach. McAdoo was one of the best shooters in NBA history. He won three straight NBA scoring titles in the 1970s as a member of the Buffalo Braves. He also averaged more than 30 points per game in each of those seasons. That was enough to get him elected into the Hall of Fame in 2000, when he was an assistant coach for Miami.

threw it into the air. For the third straight year, the Knicks had eliminated the Heat from the playoffs in Miami. And for the third straight year, the Heat were angry.

"Losing all measures up to be the same—it's bad all the time," Mourning said.

The Heat had won four straight Atlantic Division titles. But they did not have one trip to the NBA Finals to show for it. Miami's winning continued the next season, despite Mourning missing the first 69 games with a kidney disorder. Riley coached the Heat to their sixth straight playoff berth. But there would be no painfully close ending in 2001. The team lost all three games to the Charlotte Hornets in the first round by an average of 22 points.

A promising era in Heat history was over. Mourning would return to health the next year, but he would not return to form. The 2001–02 Heat struggled from beginning to end. They finished with a 36–46 record. Things went from bad to worse the following season. Still affected by his kidney ailment, Mourning did not play at all as the Heat fell to 25–57.

But a bad record often ensures a high draft choice. The Heat needed to take advantage of having the fifth overall pick in the 2003 draft. And they did just that when they landed guard

NEW HOME, NEW FRUSTRATIONS **29**

Dwyane Wade out of Marquette University.

"We feel like we have one of the best players in the draft, if not the best," Riley said after selecting Wade. "He is one of the most mature guys that I have ever met, and he is from a great college program. What I was most impressed by when I really studied him, aside from being a great defender, is his explosiveness and ability to get to the rim and score."

Riley would not coach Wade, though. He stunned the NBA world by taking over as Miami's team president and promoting assistant coach Stan Van Gundy to head coach. Wade started slowly as the Heat stumbled to a 5–15 record early in the 2003–04 season. But as he improved, so did the team.

Dandy Deal

The Heat added a talented player when they received Eddie Jones from the Charlotte Hornets in 2000. And it came as no surprise. The 6-foot-6 guard had performed well with the Hornets and the Lakers. He averaged approximately 18 points per game in each of his first four seasons with the Heat. He also was among the best three-point shooters in the NBA.

They climbed into the playoff chase by winning 12 of 15 games in March. They secured a spot in the postseason with a 42–40 record.

Though the Heat lost in the second round of the playoffs to the Indiana Pacers, they now had a player that they could build around. And after the season, the Heat acquired a center who had already been a superstar for many years—Shaquille O'Neal.

The Heat and coach Pat Riley, *right*, chose Dwyane Wade, *left*, with the fifth overall selection of the 2003 NBA Draft.

NEW HOME, NEW FRUSTRATIONS

CHAPTER 5

HELP FOR WADE: "THE DECISION"

The Heat believed Dwyane Wade was going to grow into greatness. They also believed that they were not going to win a title without replacing Alonzo Mourning with another great center.

So in 2004, they traded forwards Caron Butler, Lamar Odom, and Brian Grant, along with a first-round and second-round draft pick, to the Los Angeles Lakers for superstar center Shaquille O'Neal.

"Today the Miami Heat took a giant step forward in our continued pursuit of an NBA championship," team president

Life after Miami

Forwards Caron Butler and Lamar Odom have performed well since being traded to the Los Angeles Lakers for Shaquille O'Neal. Butler kept achieving after leaving Los Angeles and joining the Washington Wizards and then the Dallas Mavericks. He scored more than 19 points per game from 2005 to 2009. Odom became a valuable player on the Lakers' NBA title teams of 2009 and 2010.

The Heat traded for Shaquille O'Neal, *left*, and immediately became championship contenders.

HELP FOR WADE: "THE DECISION"   33

SHAQ ATTACK

One might have believed the 2006 NBA title was the last hurrah for Heat center Shaquille O'Neal. At age 38, few would have expected him to still be playing when he announced his retirement after the 2010–11 season. Though O'Neal had slowed down considerably, he played with three teams after being traded by Miami in 2008. He helped the Phoenix Suns and the Cleveland Cavaliers reach the playoffs, and he signed with the Boston Celtics in 2010.

O'Neal is one of the most dominant centers the game has seen. He averaged at least 21 points and 10 rebounds per game in each of his first 13 seasons. He led the league in scoring in 1995 and 2000, and he finished first in the NBA in shooting percentage 10 times. He made at least 57 percent of his shots in each of those years. O'Neal has also won four championships.

Pat Riley said after completing the deal. "We feel that we have traded for the best player in the NBA. You don't get many chances to acquire the best player in the league."

O'Neal and Wade transformed the Heat into a championship contender in the 2004–05 season. Wade averaged 24 points and seven assists per game. O'Neal contributed 23 points and 10 rebounds per game. Even though O'Neal missed the last month of the season with a thigh injury, the Heat still finished with the best record in the Eastern Conference at 59–23.

The Heat appeared unstoppable. They swept both the New Jersey Nets and the Washington Wizards in eight straight playoff games. Miami was on the verge of an NBA Finals berth when it took a

Heat forward Udonis Haslem, *right*, defends against Pistons center Ben Wallace during Game 3 of the 2005 Eastern Conference finals.

3–2 series lead against the Detroit Pistons. But a rib injury sidelined Wade in Game 6. The result was a lopsided loss to set up a showdown in Game 7 for the Eastern Conference title.

In Game 7, Wade combined with O'Neal for 47 points, but the rest of the team scored just 35. Wade did not score in the last 15 minutes of the game. The result was an 88–82 defeat. Wade was asked after the game why he played when he was in pain.

"Anybody in my situation would do the same thing, try to gut it out," he said. "It came

HELP FOR WADE: "THE DECISION"

Even with superstar guard Dwyane Wade, the Heat won just 15 games during the 2007–08 season.

down to the end, [Detroit] making plays. And we didn't."

In 2005–06, Pat Riley returned as head coach, and the Heat made all the right plays to win the NBA title. But injuries and age began catching up with the team the following year. O'Neal began the 2006–07 season with a knee injury that knocked him out for more than 30 games. Meanwhile, Wade was sidelined with a wrist problem.

Even Riley missed time with hip and back ailments. That, too, was a tough loss to overcome. After all, Riley was one of the finest coaches in the league.

The Heat did not live up to their nickname early that season. They were ice cold. They raised the championship banner before the opening game, and then lost by a whopping 42 points to the Chicago Bulls. Miami was limping along with an 18–23 record when O'Neal returned. They heated up briefly. But on the day Riley came back, Wade, who had finally overcome his wrist injury, dislocated his left shoulder. He left the arena in a wheelchair.

Wade had a decision to make. He could either opt for surgery, which would end his season, or he could strengthen his shoulder without surgery and hope to return for the playoffs. That is, if the Heat even made the postseason. He opted for the latter.

Thanks to O'Neal, Miami not only made the playoffs,

Not What They Had in Mind

The Heat earned a dubious record when they lost four straight games to the Chicago Bulls to open the 2007 playoffs. It marked the first time in 50 years that a defending NBA champion failed to win a game in the first round of the next postseason. Previously, the 1957 Philadelphia Warriors were swept by the Syracuse Nationals after capturing the title the season before.

but they won the Southeast Division. During a nine-game winning streak, O'Neal averaged 21 points and nine rebounds per game. Wade made it back for the playoffs, but he was not in peak form. The Heat were knocked out by the Bulls in the first round in four games.

Miami played much worse during the 2007–08 season. O'Neal performed poorly and was traded to the Phoenix Suns. Wade still had not fully recovered from his injury. The Heat's

15–67 record was the worst in the NBA.

That disaster spurred an overhaul. Riley returned to the franchise as team president and named Erik Spoelstra the new coach. The terrible record allowed the Heat to select forward Michael Beasley second overall in the NBA Draft. But he did not play well and was traded to the Minnesota Timberwolves before the 2010–11 season. The Heat then dealt for center Jermaine O'Neal, who also performed poorly.

Wade once again had little help. He led the Heat to the 2009 playoffs, but Miami again lost in the first round. The same story played out the next year with another first-round loss, this time to the Boston Celtics.

Something had to be done. After the 2010 season, Riley looked to sign free agents—players who are free to go to any team. But he had to stay within the NBA's guidelines. The league only allows teams to pay each player a certain amount. The league also enforces a salary cap. That prevents teams from paying all of their players combined more than is allowed.

The Heat decided to let go of some of its players so the team could pay the maximum salary allowed by the NBA to two new free agents. Riley set his sights on Toronto Raptors forward Chris Bosh and Cleveland Cavaliers superstar forward LeBron James. He also wanted to bring back Wade, who was now a free agent.

The Heat signed Bosh and Wade to five-year contracts on July 7, 2010. The basketball world then waited for James. He kept teams and fans anxious by announcing he would make his choice on national TV the following night. The one-hour

Dwyane Wade, *left*, Chris Bosh, *center*, and LeBron James, *right*, greet fans at a welcome party at AmericanAirlines Arena in 2010.

special was simply called "The Decision." When James finally told the world where he was headed, Heat fans jumped for joy.

"This fall I'm going to take my talents to South Beach and join the Miami Heat," he said. Telling the world on sports network ESPN that he was leaving Cleveland for Miami angered Cavaliers fans. But Heat fans were thrilled.

After all of the hoopla, the Heat started the season only 9–8. It was the beginning of an up-and-down season in Miami. The team followed its rough start by winning 21 of its next 22 games. But as the three superstars learned to play together, Miami struggled at stretches throughout the season. The team lost five of six games during a stretch in January and lost five straight in February and March.

As expected, Bosh, James, and Wade led the Heat. James averaged a team-high 26.7 points and seven assists per game. Wade added 25.5 points per game, while Bosh averaged 18.7 points and a team-high 8.3 rebounds. However, some worried that the team relied too much on those three players. Forward Udonis Haslem was the team's fourth highest scorer, but he averaged only eight points per game.

Despite the questions surrounding the team, Miami finished 58–24, which was good enough for the second seed in the Eastern Conference playoffs. And with the three stars leading the way, the Heat quickly became the most feared team in the league. Miami handily beat the Philadelphia 76ers and Boston Celtics, winning each series four games to one. Even the top-seeded Chicago Bulls were no challenge for the Heat in the conference finals. Miami won that series 4–1 as well.

That set up a rematch of the 2006 NBA Finals between the Heat and the Dallas Mavericks. Many thought the Heat would also roll through the Mavericks and win another

> **King James**
>
> Heat fans had every right to be excited by the signing of LeBron James in 2010. His greatness on the court has earned him the nickname "King James." James averaged 20.9 points per game as a rookie and kept getting better. He scored at least 27 points per game in each of the next six years. And he led the league at 30 points per game in his fifth season. James was named NBA MVP in 2009 and 2010.

The Heat's LeBron James (6) goes up for a shot against the Dallas Mavericks' Tyson Chandler in Game 5 of the 2011 NBA Finals.

NBA title. They started out well, winning two of the first three games. But then the Heat began to struggle. James had trouble scoring late in games. Meanwhile, Wade suffered a bruised hip early in Game 5. Behind forward Dirk Nowitzki, Dallas took the next three games and the NBA title.

It was a disappointing ending to an exciting season in Miami. But with three of the game's top superstars wearing Miami Heat uniforms, fans had little doubt that their team would be contending for more titles in the years to come.

TIMELINE

1987	The NBA announces on April 22 that it is adding four teams, including one in Miami.
1988	The Miami Heat make their debut on November 5 and lose to the Los Angeles Clippers 111–91. A crowd of 15,008 is in attendance at Miami Arena. After 17 straight losses, the Heat earn their first win on December 14 by beating the Clippers 89–88.
1992	The Heat lose their first-ever playoff game to the Chicago Bulls on April 24. The defeat is the first of three in a sweep.
1994	The Heat win a playoff game for the first time by beating the Atlanta Hawks on April 28. They lose the series in five games.
1995	Pat Riley is hired as team president and coach on September 2 and quickly establishes himself as the most successful coach in franchise history. The Heat trade top player Glen Rice on November 3 in a deal that brings in center Alonzo Mourning.
1996	Guard Tim Hardaway is acquired in a trade on February 22.
1997	The Heat complete a second-round playoff series victory over the New York Knicks on May 18 with a 101–90 win. The two series wins are the first in franchise history.

MIAMI HEAT

2000	On May 21, an 83–82 loss to New York in Game 7 of the second round clinches a third straight playoff loss to the Knicks.
2003	The Heat select guard Dwyane Wade with the fifth pick of the NBA Draft on June 26.
2004	Forwards Caron Butler, Lamar Odom, and Brian Grant and two draft picks are sent to the Los Angeles Lakers on July 14. In return, the Heat acquire superstar center Shaquille O'Neal.
2005	A rib injury to Wade proves costly as the Heat lose to the Detroit Pistons in Game 7 of the Eastern Conference Finals 88–82 on June 6.
2006	The Heat clinch their first NBA championship on June 20 with a 95–92 win over the Dallas Mavericks. The Game 7 victory is their fourth straight after losing the first two games of the series.
2008	The struggling Heat trade O'Neal to the Phoenix Suns on February 6. The Heat bottom out with a 15–67 record for the season.
2010	The Heat sign free agents LeBron James and Chris Bosh to five-year contracts on July 7.
2011	The Heat advance to the NBA Finals and again face the Dallas Mavericks. This time, they lose to the Mavericks four games to two.

QUICK STATS

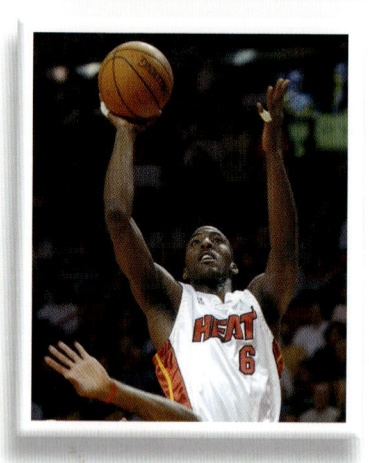

FRANCHISE HISTORY
Miami Heat (1988–)

NBA FINALS
(win in bold)

2006, 2011

CONFERENCE FINALS
1997, 2005, 2006, 2011

DIVISION CHAMPIONSHIPS
1997, 1998, 1999, 2000, 2005, 2006, 2007, 2011

KEY PLAYERS
(position; years with team)

Chris Bosh (F; 2010–)
Sherman Douglas (G; 1989–92)
Kevin Edwards (G; 1988–93)
Tim Hardaway (G; 1996–2001)
LeBron James (F; 2010–)
Eddie Jones (G; 2000–05, 2007)
Jamal Mashburn (F; 1997–2000)
Alonzo Mourning (C; 1995–2002, 2005–08)
Shaquille O'Neal (C; 2004–08)
Gary Payton (G; 2005–07)
Glen Rice (F; 1989–95)
Rony Seikaly (C; 1988–94)
Steve Smith (G; 1991–94, 2005)
Dwyane Wade (G; 2003–)

KEY COACHES
Kevin Loughery (1991–95): 133–159; 2–6 (postseason)
Pat Riley (1995–2003, 2005–08): 454–395; 34–36 (postseason)
Erik Spoelstra (2008–): 148–98; 18–15 (postseason)

HOME ARENAS
Miami Arena (1988–99)
AmericanAirlines Arena (2000–)

*All statistics through 2010–11 season

QUOTES AND ANECDOTES

Shaquille O'Neal is more than just a great basketball player. He also became a reserve officer for the Miami Beach police department in 2005. He took a salary of $1 a year to work for the department as a volunteer. O'Neal helped make an arrest in South Beach. He watched as a man assaulted a stranger on the street, hopped into a car, and drove away. O'Neal followed the car, and then called a police officer with its location. The man was arrested.

"I want to live 50 more years. I'm 33 years old . . . and I want to live to at least be 80 and see my kids grow up and see my grandkids. That's important to me." —Heat center Alonzo Mourning after doctors told him he should never play again because of a kidney disorder. Mourning received a kidney transplant and played several more years.

Heat forward Glen Rice was prone to offensive explosions. But he was never hotter than he was on April 15, 1995. Rice scored 56 points that night against the Orlando Magic. It was the highest single-game point total in the NBA that season. He hit an astounding 20 of 27 shots, including seven of eight from three-point range.

"Bring it on. We'll accept it. At the end of the day we know what's important. And what's important is winning ballgames and winning championships. So once you do that, winner take all." —Heat guard Dwyane Wade as the fans celebrated his return and the signings of fellow superstars LeBron James and Chris Bosh in July 2010

GLOSSARY

assist
A pass that leads directly to a made basket.

contender
A team that is in the race for a championship or playoff berth.

contract
A binding agreement about, for example, years of commitment by a basketball player in exchange for a given salary.

draft
A system used by professional sports leagues to select new players in order to spread incoming talent among all teams. The NBA Draft is held each June.

expansion
In sports, the addition of a franchise or franchises to a league.

fast break
A style of basketball in which a team runs down the court and tries to score before the opponent's defense is set.

franchise
An entire sports organization, including the players, coaches, and staff.

free agent
A player whose contract has expired and who is able to sign with a team of his choice.

layup
A shot close to the basket that is either dropped in or banked off the backboard.

playoffs
A series of games in which the winners advance in a quest to win a championship.

rebound
To secure the basketball after a missed shot.

trade
A move in which a player or players are sent from one team to another.

FOR MORE INFORMATION

Further Reading

Ballard, Chris. *The Art of a Beautiful Game: The Thinking Fan's Tour of the NBA.* New York: Simon & Schuster, 2009.

Riley, Pat. *The Winner Within: A Life Plan for Team Players.* New York: Penguin, 1993.

Simmons, Bill. *The Book of Basketball: The NBA According to the Sports Guy.* New York: Random House, 2009.

Web Links

To learn more about the Miami Heat, visit ABDO Publishing Company online at **www.abdopublishing.com**. Web sites about the Heat are featured on our Book Links page. These links are routinely monitored and updated to provide the most current information available.

Places To Visit

AmericanAirlines Arena
601 Biscayne Boulevard
Miami, FL 33132-1801
(786) 777-1000
http://www.aaarena.com/
This has been the Heat's home arena since 2000. The team plays 41 regular-season games here each year.

Florida Sports Hall of Fame
Lake Myrtle Sports Complex
905 Lake Myrtle Park Drive
Auburndale, FL 33823
863-551-4750
www.floridasportshalloffame.com
This museum provides many exhibits and memorabilia on the history of the Heat and Florida's other professional and collegiate sports teams.

Naismith Memorial Basketball Hall of Fame
1000 West Columbus Avenue
Springfield, MA 01105
413-781-6500
www.hoophall.com
This hall of fame and museum highlights the greatest players and moments in the history of basketball. Former Heat coach Pat Riley is enshrined here.

INDEX

AmericanAirlines Arena, 25
Arison, Mickey (owner), 17
Atlanta Hawks, 15, 17

Beasley, Michael, 38
Bosh, Chris, 38, 40
Boston Celtics, 6, 34, 38, 40
Butler, Caron, 33

Charlotte Hornets, 11, 13, 18, 29, 30
Chicago Bulls, 15, 20, 22, 37, 40
Cleveland Cavaliers, 15, 34, 38–39
Cunningham, Billy (owner), 12

Dallas Mavericks, 5–7, 21, 33, 40–41
Detroit Pistons, 25, 35–36
Douglas, Sherman, 12–14

Edwards, Kevin, 12

Gentry, Alvin (coach), 18
Golden State Warriors, 18
Grant, Brian, 33

Hardaway, Tim, 18, 19, 20–21, 26
Haslem, Udonis, 40

Indiana Pacers, 30

James, LeBron, 38–41
Jones, Eddie, 30

Long, Grant, 17
Los Angeles Lakers, 6, 9, 11, 28, 30, 33
Loughery, Kevin (coach), 14, 18

Mashburn, Jamal, 21
Miami Arena, 15, 22
Milwaukee Bucks, 6
Minnesota Timberwolves, 11, 13, 38
Mourning, Alonzo, 18–23, 25–26, 29, 33

NBA Finals
  2006, 5–9, 36, 40
  2011, 40–41
New Jersey Nets, 34
New York Knicks, 9, 18, 19, 21–22, 25–29

Odom, Lamar, 33
O'Neal, Jermaine, 38
O'Neal, Shaquille, 6, 23, 30, 33–37
Orlando Magic, 11, 13, 15, 21, 25

Payton, Gary, 6
Philadelphia 76ers, 12, 37, 40
Philadelphia Warriors, 37
Phoenix Suns, 34, 37

Rice, Glen, 12, 14–15, 18
Riley, Pat (coach and president), 5, 9, 18–19, 21, 28, 29–30, 34, 36–38
Rothstein, Ron (coach), 12, 14

Seattle SuperSonics, 6
Seikaly, Rony, 12–13, 14, 17
Smith, Steve, 14–15, 17
Spoelstra, Erik, 38
Syracuse Nationals, 37

Toronto Raptors, 38

Van Gundy, Stan (coach), 5, 30

Wade, Dwyane, 6–7, 9, 23, 30, 33–38, 40–41
Washington Wizards, 33, 34
Weatherspoon, Clarence, 27
Willis, Kevin, 18

About the Author

Marty Gitlin is a freelance writer based in Cleveland, Ohio. He has written more than 35 educational books. Gitlin has won more than 45 awards during his 25 years as a writer, including first place for general excellence from the Associated Press. He lives with his wife and three children.